D1095065

CALGARY PUBLIC LIBRARY

AUG   2016

Gabby
WONDER GIRL

Joyce Grant

Illustrated by Jan Dolby

Fitzhenry & Whiteside

Text copyright © 2016 Joyce Grant
Illustrations copyright © 2016 Jan Dolby

Published in Canada by Fitzhenry & Whiteside, 195 Allstate Parkway, Markham, Ontario L3R 4T8
Published in the United States in 2016 by Fitzhenry & Whiteside, 311 Washington Street, Brighton, Massachusetts 02135
All rights reserved. No part of this book may be reproduced in any manner without the express written consent of the publisher, except in the case of brief excerpts in critical reviews and articles. All inquiries should be addressed to Fitzhenry & Whiteside Limited, 195 Allstate Parkway, Markham, Ontario L3R 4T8.

www.fitzhenry.ca   godwit@fitzhenry.ca

10 9 8 7 6 5 4 3 2 1

Library and Archives Canada Cataloguing in Publication
Grant, Joyce, 1963-, author
Gabby, wonder girl / Joyce Grant ; illustrated by Jan Dolby.
(Gabby ; 3)
ISBN 978-1-55455-384-6 (bound)
I. Dolby, Jan, 1967-, illustrator II. Title.
PS8613.R3653G3342015   jC813'.6   C2015-904019-1

Publisher Cataloging-in-Publication Data (U.S.)
Grant, Joyce, 1963-
Gabby wonder girl / Joyce Grant ; illustrations by Jan Dolby.
[32] pages : color illustrations ; cm. –Gabby.
Summary: "Gabby returns as Wonder Girl in the third book of the Gabby series. When Gabby finds a mysterious photograph in her backyard, she teams up with her best friend, Super Roy, to figure out who the strange girl in the picture is. Using her magic book and the power of punctuation, Gabby and Roy must ask the right question to solve the mystery and save the day" – Provided by publisher.
ISBN: 978-1-55455-384-6
1. Mystery and detective stories. 2. Magic – Juvenile fiction.   I. Dolby, Jan. II. Title. III. Series.
[E] dc23 PZ7.1.G735Wo 2015

Fitzhenry & Whiteside acknowledges with thanks the Canada Council for the Arts, and the Ontario Arts Council for their support of our publishing program. We acknowledge the financial support of the Government of Canada through the Canada Book Fund (CBF) for our publishing activities.

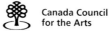

Cover and interior design by Daniel Choi
Cover image by Jan Dolby
Printed in Hong Kong by Paramount Printing Company Ltd.

This book is for all of the Wonder Girls.
This book is for *you*.
—J.G.

For my hero, Jack.
—J.D.

We wish to thank Grand Chief Eddie Erasmus,
Tlicho government, and Dr. John B. Zoe, Senior
Advisor to the Tlicho government, for their
invaluable assistance and guidance.
Thank you also to Dale Matasawagon of the
Assembly of First Nations.

Today, Gabby was...**WONDER GIRL**!

She scanned the backyard with her super-vision, looking for her sidekick, Roy.

Wait! What was that?

Gabby picked up the photograph.

Who is this little girl named Greta? she wondered. Maybe Roy would know.

"Roy!" she called out.

A voice from a pile of squiggles called back. "Gaaaaaaa-bby!"

"I'll save you, Roy!" said Gabby.

Greta

Gabby ran—so strong and so fast,

she was practically a blur.

When she got to Roy, Gabby saw that he was stuck in the squiggles. She looked more closely. "These are *question marks*, Roy!"

"What are they for?" asked Roy, as Gabby helped him out.

"They help you ask questions," she answered. "Where did they come from?"

"I shook your magic book to get some letters and they fell out."

"You don't shake the book to get letters," said Gabby. "You…smash it!"

Gabby launched the book.

Letters flew everywhere!

Roy removed a messy m from the mud
and added an a from around his ankle,
an s that was stuck on his shirt, and a k
from the kite.

Poof!

It spelled **mask**.

Roy immediately felt stronger—and more stylish!

"We have a mystery to solve, Super Roy!" said Gabby. "Do you know this girl?"

Greta

"No, but she looks familiar," said Roy. "I wonder who she is."

"Who!" said Gabby. "That's a question word! We can use a question mark to figure this out."

Gabby waved a white w, the hedgehog held an h, and the owl offered an o. Gabby put the letters together to spell **who**.

"This word isn't helping," said Roy. "It isn't telling us who the little girl in the picture is."

"Wait," said Gabby. "Watch what happens when we add…"

...a question mark."

The question shimmered and shone
and gradually became...

"Mrs. Oldham's butterflies! The girl in the picture is Mrs. Oldham!" cried Gabby.

The dynamic duo ran over to the fence and peered into the backyard of Gabby's neighbour. "Mrs. Oldham!" they called. There was no answer.

"I wonder where she is," said Gabby.

They looked at each other. "Where!" they cried. "That's a great question."

A w wafted in on the wind.

Roy found an h half-hidden in the hammock...

an e in the electric car...

an r resting on the race track...

and another teeny-tiny e on his elbow.

He added a question mark.

The question got bigger. It shivered and shook and turned into…

"Mrs. Oldham is in the apple tree!"
they shouted.

They ran over to Mrs. Oldham's yard
and found her snagged on a branch.

"Mrs. Oldham, what are you doing?" asked Gabby.

"Picking apples to make a pie, just like when I was a little girl," said Mrs. Oldham.

"It's you in the picture!" cried Gabby.

"Yes!" said Mrs. Oldham. "Thank you for finding my old photograph."

"How are we going to get her down?" asked Roy.

Gabby knew how. She gathered an h, an o, and a w.

But what was missing?

Roy ran to get a question mark.

"Oh no!" he cried. "The hedgehog has chewed up every last one of them! What will we do now?"

Suddenly, the slithery snake did something strange.

how became a question!

How could they help Mrs. Oldham?

As they watched, the **how?** shuddered and shimmied and turned into…

...a ladder.

"That's how we'll get her down," said Gabby.

Gabby the Wonder Girl and Super Roy found a ladder in the yard. Gabby carefully climbed up and rescued Mrs. Oldham.

When she was safely on the ground, Mrs. Oldham plucked a **p** from the poppies, inserted an **i** that was inside the inuksuk, and ended with an **e** from the elf to make...

...a delicious **pie**.

"Who wants a slice?"
asked Mrs. Oldham.

"We thought you'd never ask," said Gabby.

k

Here are some helpful Question Words

Who?

What?

When?

Where?

Why?

Which?

Whose?

How?

Use these question words to create some questions about these pictures:

Fun Gabby: Wonder Girl Activities–*For You!*

Word Scramble
Unscramble the words below!

Answers: car tree hedgehog apple pie snake

How to Draw **Mrs. Oldham**

Draw:
- an oval for her head
- a rectangle for her body
- a smaller rectangle for her skirt
- two thin rectangles for her legs
- two ovals for her feet.

Add:
- two circles for her ears
- two triangles for her arms
- two ovals for her hands
- a half circle for her hair band.

Add:
- crazy hair
- lines for her robe and skirt
- her slippers.

Add:
- sunglasses
- polka dots on her hair band and robe
- her eyes, eyelashes, nose, lips.
- Don't forget her butterflies!

ABCDEFGHIJKLMNOPQRSTUVWXYZ

Wonderful Question Games
You Can Play With Your Friends!

Answer a Question with a Question

Here's a silly game you can play on a long car ride.

One person starts by asking a question. For instance, "Where is your hat?"

The next person answers—with a question. For instance, "Why do you want to know?"

Each person has to answer the question with a question: "Who says I want to know?"

The game is over when someone accidentally answers with a statement.

The remaining players can keep going until the next person is out, or you can simply start the game over again with a different question.

Guessing Game

Here's a great game for two or more people.

- One person thinks of an object in the room.
  - The other players take turns asking questions that can be answered with either "yes" or "no" and try to guess what the object is.

For instance:

"Is it orange?"

"Is it on the floor?"

- The first person to guess the object wins and gets to choose the next object.

abcdefghijklmnopqrstuvwxyz

Gabby is Online

Visit the author's website at **joycegrantauthor.com** and the illustrator's website at **jandolby.com** for great Gabby news, information, games and a kids' art gallery. Download a free teacher's guide at: **http://joycegrantauthor.com/free-teachers-guide-gabby/**

Look! An inuksuk!

In her backyard, Mrs. Oldham has a small inuksuk (pronounced "in-ook-shook"). An inuksuk is a stone marker used by North America's northern Aboriginal people to help travellers. Did you know that Nunavut's flag has an inuksuk on it?

Find the Hedgehog

On nearly every page, the hedgehog is holding a letter. Put them all together to spell two words that are important to this story.

Answer: question mark

Check out the
other books in the
Gabby series!

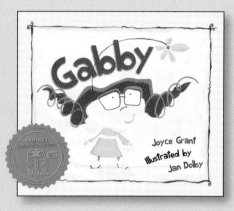

Praise for *Gabby*:

- 2015 Rainforest of Reading winner (Montserrat)
- 2014 Rainforest of Reading nominee (St. Lucia, Grenada)
- 2014 Toy Testing Council Recommended Read
- 2013 Ontario Library Association Top 10 Best Bets
- 2013 Canadian Children's Book Centre's Best Books for Kids and Teens

"*Gabby* is a colourful and animated picture book that will engage children through its bright illustrations and imaginative text. The story also functions as a creative lesson in how to spell and attach meaning to words."
—*CM Magazine*

"A charming read-aloud story ideal for getting little ones interested in forming their own spelled-out words. Highly recommended."
—*Midwest Book Review (The Picturebook Shelf)*

"Look at this little cutie! Could it be a junior Pippi? No, this little one is Gabby and she's much more grounded and responsible, but still imaginative."
—*CanLit For Little Canadians*

"The connection between words and the real things they represent is playfully presented in this first book by journalist and editor Joyce Grant."
—*City Parent, On The Bookshelf*